Dedicated to Joanna Pilkington,
who found fairies in her
beautiful garden

Special thanks to
Narinder Dhami

ORCHARD BOOKS
338 Euston Road, London NW1 3BH
Orchard Books Australia
Level 17/207 Kent Street, Sydney, NSW 2000
A Paperback Original

First published in 2003 by Orchard Books.

HiT entertainment

A CIP catalogue record for this book is available
from the British Library.

ISBN 978 1 84362 016 7

51

Printed in Great Britain

Orchard Books is a division of Hachette Children's Books,
an Hachette UK company

www.hachette.co.uk

Ruby,
the Red
Fairy

by Daisy Meadows

illustrated by Georgie Ripper

ORCHARD

The Fairyland Palace

Maze

Forest

Orchard

Black Pot

Meadow

Tower

Beach

Rockpools

Rainspell Island

Jack Frost's
Ice Castle

Tom Goodfellow's
House

Merry-go-round

Mrs Merry's
Cottage

Willow
Tree

Stream

Field

Mermaid
Cottage

Town

Harbour

Dolphin Cottage

Cold winds blow and thick ice form,
I conjure up this fairy storm.
To seven corners of the mortal world
the Rainbow Fairies will be hurled!

I curse every part of Fairyland,
with a frosty wave of my icy hand.
For now and always, from this fateful day,
Fairyland will be cold and grey!

Contents

The End of the Rainbow

"Look, Dad!" said Rachel Walker. She pointed across the blue-green sea at the rocky island ahead of them. The ferry was sailing towards it, dipping up and down on the rolling waves. "Is that Rainspell Island?" she asked.

Her dad nodded. "Yes, it is," he said, smiling. "Our holiday is about to begin!"

The waves slapped against the side
of the ferry as it bobbed up and down
on the water. Rachel felt her heart
thump with excitement. She could see
white cliffs and emerald green fields on
the island. And golden sandy beaches,
with rock pools dotted here and there.

Suddenly, a few fat raindrops
plopped down on to Rachel's head.
"Oh!" she gasped, surprised. The sun
was still shining.

Rachel's mum grabbed her hand. "Let's get under cover," she said, leading Rachel inside.

"Isn't that strange?" Rachel said. "Sunshine *and* rain!"

"Let's hope the rain stops before we get off the ferry," said Mr Walker. "Now, where did I put that map of the island?"

Rachel looked out of the window. Her eyes opened wide.

A girl was standing alone on the deck. Her dark hair was wet with raindrops, but she didn't seem to care. She just stared up at the sky.

Rachel looked over at her mum and dad. They were busy studying the map. So Rachel slipped back outside to see what was so interesting.

And there it was.

In the blue sky, high above them, was the most amazing rainbow that Rachel had ever seen. One end of the rainbow was far out to sea. The other seemed to fall somewhere on Rainspell Island. All of the colours were bright and clear.

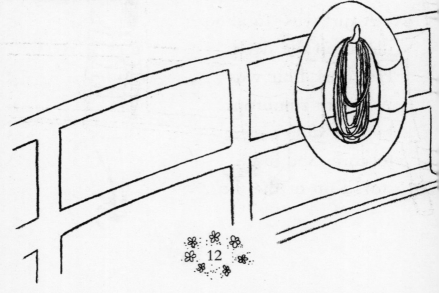

Red,
orange,
yellow,
green,
blue,
indigo
and violet.

"Isn't it perfect?" the dark-haired girl whispered to Rachel.

"Yes, it is," Rachel agreed. "Are you going to Rainspell on holiday?"

The girl nodded. "We're staying for a week," she said. "I'm Kirsty Tate."

Rachel smiled, as the rain began to stop. "I'm Rachel Walker. We're staying at Mermaid Cottage," she added.

"And we're at Dolphin Cottage," said Kirsty. "Do you think we might be near each other?"

"I hope so," Rachel replied. She had a feeling she was going to like Kirsty.

Kirsty leaned over the rail and looked down into the shimmering water. "The sea looks really deep, doesn't it?" she said. "There might even be mermaids down there, watching us right now!"

Rachel stared at the waves. She saw
something that made her heart skip a
beat. "Look!" she said. "Is that a
mermaid's hair?" Then she laughed,
when she saw that it was just seaweed.

"It could be a mermaid's necklace,"
said Kirsty, smiling. "Maybe she lost
it when she was trying to escape from
a sea monster."

The ferry was now sailing into Rainspell's tiny harbour. Seagulls flew around them, and fishing boats bobbed on the water.

"Look at that big white cliff over there," Kirsty said. She pointed it out to Rachel. "It looks a bit like a giant's face, doesn't it?" Rachel looked, and nodded. Kirsty seemed to see magic *everywhere*.

"There you are,
Rachel!" called Mrs
Walker. Rachel turned
round and saw her
mum and dad coming
out on to the deck.
"We'll be getting off the
ferry in a few minutes,"
Mrs Walker added.

"Mum, Dad, this is Kirsty," Rachel
said. "She's staying at Dolphin Cottage."

"That's right next door to ours," said
Mr Walker. "I remember seeing it on
the map."

Rachel and Kirsty looked at each
other in delight.

"I'd better go and find *my* mum and
dad," said Kirsty. She looked round.
"Oh, here they are."

Kirsty's mum and dad came over
to say hello to the Walkers. Then the
ferry docked, and everyone began to
leave the boat.

"Our cottages are on the other side
of the harbour," said Rachel's dad,
looking at the map. "It's not far."

Mermaid Cottage and Dolphin
Cottage were right next to the beach.
Rachel loved her bedroom, which was
high up, in the attic. From the
window, she could see the waves
rolling onto the sand.

A shout from outside made her look down. It was Kirsty. She was standing under the window, waving at her.

"Let's go and explore the beach!" Kirsty called.

Rachel dashed outside to join her.

Seaweed lay in piles on the sand, and there were tiny pink and white shells dotted about.

"I love it here already!" Rachel shouted happily above the noise of the seagulls.

"Me too," Kirsty said. She pointed up at the sky. "Look, the rainbow's still there."

Rachel looked up. The rainbow glowed brightly among the fluffy white clouds.

"Have you heard the story about the pot of gold at the end of the rainbow?" Kirsty asked.

Rachel nodded. "Yes, but that's just in fairy stories," she said.

Kirsty grinned. "Maybe. But let's go and find out for ourselves!"

"OK," Rachel agreed. "We can explore the island at the same time."

They rushed back to tell their parents
where they were going. Then Kirsty
and Rachel set off along a lane behind
the cottages. It led them away from the
beach, across green fields, and towards
a small wood.

Rachel kept looking up at the rainbow. She was worried that it would start to fade now that the rain had stopped. But the colours stayed clear and bright.

"It looks like the end of the rainbow is over there," Kirsty said. "Come on!" And she hurried towards the trees.

The wood was cool and green after the heat of the sun. Rachel and Kirsty followed a winding path until they came to a clearing. Then they both stopped and stared.

The rainbow shone down on to the grass through a gap in the trees.

And there, at the rainbow's end, lay an old, black pot.

A Tiny Surprise

"Look!" Kirsty whispered. "There really is a pot of gold!"

"It could just be a cooking pot," Rachel said doubtfully. "Some campers might have left it behind."

But Kirsty shook her head. "I don't think so," she said. "It looks really old."

Rachel stared at the pot. It was sitting on the grass, upside down.

"Let's have a closer look," said Kirsty. She ran to the pot and tried to turn it over. "Oh, it's heavy!" she gasped. She tried again, but the pot didn't move.

Rachel rushed to help her. They both pushed and pushed at the pot. This time it moved, just a little.

"Let's try again," Kirsty panted. "Are you ready, Rachel?"

Tap! Tap! Tap!

Rachel and Kirsty stared at each other.

"What was that?" Rachel gasped.

"I don't know," whispered Kirsty.

Tap! Tap!

"There it is again," Kirsty said. She looked down at the pot lying on the grass. "You know what? I think it's coming from inside this pot!"

Rachel's eyes opened wide. "Are you sure?" She bent down, and put her ear to the pot. *Tap! Tap!* Then, to her amazement, Rachel heard a tiny voice.

"Help!" it called. "Help me!"

Rachel grabbed Kirsty's arm. "Did you hear that?" she asked.

Kirsty nodded. "Quick!" she said. "We *must* turn the pot over!"

Rachel and Kirsty pushed at the pot as hard as they could. It began to rock from side to side on the grass.

"We're nearly there!" Rachel panted. "Keep pushing, Kirsty!"

The girls pushed with all their might. Suddenly, the pot turned over and rolled on to its side. Rachel and Kirsty were taken by surprise. They both lost their balance and landed on the grass with a thump.

"Look!" Kirsty whispered, breathing hard.

A small shower of sparkling red dust had flown out of the pot. Rachel and Kirsty gasped with surprise. The dust hung in the air above them. And there, right in the middle of the glittering cloud, was a tiny winged girl.

Rachel and Kirsty watched in wonder as the tiny girl fluttered in the sunlight, her delicate wings sparkling with all the colours of the rainbow.

"Oh, Rachel!" Kirsty whispered. "It's a fairy…"

Fairy Magic

The fairy flew over Rachel and Kirsty's heads. Her short, silky dress was the colour of ripe strawberries. Red crystal earrings glowed in her ears. Her golden hair was plaited with tiny red roses, and her little feet wore crimson slippers.

She waved her scarlet wand, and the shower of sparkling red fairy dust

floated softly down to the ground.
Where it landed, all sorts of red flowers
appeared with a *pop!*

Rachel and Kirsty watched
open-mouthed. It really and truly *was*
a fairy.

"This is like a dream," Rachel said.

"I always believed in fairies," Kirsty
whispered back. "But I never thought
I'd ever *see* one!"

The fairy flew towards them. "Oh,
thank you *so* much!" she called in a
tiny, silvery voice. "I'm free at last!"
She glided down, and landed on
Kirsty's hand.

Kirsty gasped. The fairy felt lighter
and softer than a butterfly.

"I was beginning to think I'd *never*
get out of the pot!" the fairy said.

Kirsty wanted to ask the fairy so
many things. But she didn't know
where to start.

"Tell me your names, quickly," said
the fairy. She fluttered up into the air
again. "There's so much to be done,
and we must get started right away."

Rachel wondered what the fairy meant. "I'm Rachel," she said.

"And I'm Kirsty," said Kirsty. "But who are *you?*"

"I'm the Red Rainbow Fairy – but call me Ruby," the fairy replied.

"Ruby..." Kirsty breathed. "A Rainbow Fairy..." She and Rachel stared at each other in excitement. This really *was* magic!

"Yes," said Ruby. "And I have six sisters: Amber, Saffron, Fern, Sky, Izzy and Heather. One for each colour of the rainbow, you see."

"What do Rainbow Fairies do?"
Rachel asked.

Ruby flew over and landed lightly on
Rachel's hand. "It's our job to put all the
different colours into Fairyland," she
explained.

"So why were you shut up inside
that old pot?" asked Rachel.

"And where are your sisters?" Kirsty
added.

Ruby's golden wings drooped. Her
eyes filled with tiny, sparkling tears.
"I don't know," she said. "Something
terrible has happened in Fairyland. We
really need your help!"

Fairies in Danger

Kirsty stared down at Ruby, sitting sadly on Rachel's hand. "Of course we'll help you!" she said.

"Just tell us how," added Rachel.

Ruby wiped the tears from her eyes. "Thank you!" she said. "But first I must show you the terrible thing that has happened. Follow me – as quickly as you can!" She flew into the air, her wings shimmering in the sunshine.

Rachel and Kirsty followed Ruby across the clearing. She danced ahead of them, glowing like a crimson flame. She stopped at a small pond under a weeping willow tree. "Look! I can show you what happened yesterday," she said.

She flew over the pond and scattered another shower of sparkling fairy dust with her tiny, red wand. At once, the water lit up with a strange, silver light. It bubbled and fizzed, and then became still. With wide eyes, Rachel and Kirsty watched as a picture appeared. It was like looking through a window into another land!

"Oh, Rachel, look!" said Kirsty.

A river of brightest blue ran swiftly past hills of greenest green. Scattered on the hillsides were red and white toadstool houses. And on top of the highest hill stood a silver palace with four pink towers.

The towers were so high, their points were almost hidden by the fluffy white clouds floating past.

Hundreds of fairies were making their way towards the palace. Some were walking and some were flying. Rachel and Kirsty could see goblins, elves, imps and pixies too. Everyone seemed very excited.

"Yesterday was the day of the Fairyland Midsummer Ball," Ruby explained. She flew over the pond and pointed down with her wand to a spot in the middle of the scene. "There I am, with my Rainbow sisters."

Kirsty and Rachel looked closely at where Ruby was pointing. They saw seven fairies, each dressed prettily in their own rainbow colour. Wherever

they flew, they left a trail of fairy dust
behind them.

"The Midsummer Ball is *very*
special," Ruby went on. "And my
sisters and I are always in charge of
sending out invitations."

To the sound of tinkling music, the front doors of the palace slowly opened. "Here come King Oberon and Queen Titania," said Ruby. "The Fairy King and Queen. They are about to begin the ball."

Kirsty and Rachel watched as the King and Queen stepped out. The King wore a splendid golden coat and golden crown. His queen wore a silver dress and a tiara that sparkled with diamonds. Everyone cheered loudly. After a while, the King signalled for quiet. "Fairies," he began. "We are very glad to see you all here. Welcome to the Midsummer Ball!"

The fairies clapped their hands and cheered again. A band of green frogs in smart purple outfits started to play, and the dancing began.

Suddenly, a grey mist seemed to fill the room. Kirsty and Rachel watched in alarm as all the fairies started to shiver. And a loud, chilly voice shouted out, "Stop the music!"

The band fell silent. Everyone looked scared. A tall, bony figure was pushing his way through the crowd. He was dressed all in white, and there was frost on his white hair and beard. Icicles hung from his clothes. But his face was red and angry.

"Who's that?" Rachel asked with a shiver. Ice had begun to form around the edge of the pond.

"It's Jack Frost," said Ruby. And she shivered too.

Jack Frost glared at the seven Rainbow Fairies. "Why wasn't I invited to the Midsummer Ball?" he asked coldly.

The Rainbow Fairies gasped in horror...

Ruby looked up from the pond picture. She smiled sadly at Rachel and Kirsty. "Yes, we forgot to invite Jack Frost," she said.

The Fairy Queen stepped forward. "You are very welcome, Jack Frost," she said. "Please stay and enjoy the ball."

But Jack Frost looked even more
angry. "Too late!" he hissed. "You
forgot to invite me!" He turned and
pointed a thin, icy finger at the
Rainbow Fairies.

"Well, you will not forget this!" he went on. "My spell will banish the Rainbow Fairies to the seven corners of the mortal world. From this day on, Fairyland will be without colour – for ever!"

Jack Frost's Spell

As Jack Frost cast his spell, a great, icy wind began to blow. It picked up the seven Rainbow Fairies and spun them up into the darkening sky. The other fairies watched in dismay.

Jack Frost turned to the King and Queen. "Your Rainbow Fairies will be trapped, never to return." With that, he left, leaving a trail of icy footprints.

Quickly, the Fairy Queen stepped forward and lifted her silver wand. "I cannot undo Jack Frost's magic completely," she shouted, as the wind howled and rushed around her. "But I can guide the Rainbow Fairies to a safe place until they can be rescued!"

The Queen pointed her wand at the

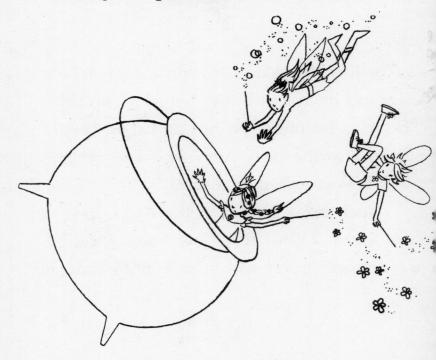

grey sky overhead. A black pot came
spinning through the stormy clouds. It
flew towards the Rainbow Fairies. One
by one, the Rainbow Fairies tumbled
into the pot.

"Pot-at-the-end-of-the-rainbow, keep
our Rainbow Fairies safely together,"
the Queen called. "And take them to
Rainspell Island!"

The pot flew out of sight, behind a dark cloud. And the bright colours of Fairyland began to fade, until it looked like an old black and white photograph.

"Oh no!" Kirsty gasped. Then the picture in the pond vanished.

"So the Fairy Queen cast her *own* spell!" Rachel said. She was bursting with questions. "She put you and your sisters in the pot, and sent you to Rainspell."

Ruby nodded. "Our Queen knew that we would be safe here," she said. "We know Rainspell well. It is a place full of magic."

"But where are your sisters?" Kirsty wanted to know. "They were in the pot too."

Ruby looked upset. "Jack Frost's spell must have been stronger than the Queen thought," she said. "As the pot spun through the sky, the wind blew my sisters out again. I was at the bottom, so I was safe. But I was trapped when the pot landed upside down."

"So are your sisters somewhere on Rainspell?" Kirsty asked.

Ruby nodded. "Yes, but they're scattered all over the island. Jack Frost's spell has trapped them too." She flew towards Kirsty and landed on her shoulder. "That's where you and Rachel come in."

"How?" Rachel asked.

"You found *me*, didn't you?" the fairy went on. "That's because you believe in magic." She flew from Kirsty's shoulder to Rachel's. "So, you could rescue my Rainbow sisters too! Then we can all bring colour back to Fairyland again."

A Visit to Fairyland

"Of course we'll search for your sisters,"
Kirsty said quickly. "Won't we,
Rachel?"

Rachel nodded.

"Oh, thank you," Ruby said happily.

"But we're only here for a week,"
Rachel said. "Will that be long enough?"

"We must get started right away,"

said Ruby. "First, I must take you to
Fairyland to meet our King and
Queen. They will be very pleased to
know that you are going to help me
find my sisters."

Rachel and Kirsty stared at Ruby.

"You're taking us to *Fairyland?*"
Kirsty gasped. She could hardly believe
her ears. Nor could Rachel.

"But how will we get there?" Rachel
wanted to know.

"We'll fly there," Ruby replied.

"But *we* can't fly!" Rachel pointed
out.

Ruby smiled. She whirled up into
the air and flew over the girls'
heads. Then she swirled her wand
above them. Magic red fairy dust
fluttered down.

Rachel and Kirsty began to feel a bit strange. Were the trees getting bigger or were they getting smaller?

They were getting smaller!

Smaller and smaller and smaller, until they were the same size as Ruby.

"I'm tiny!" Rachel laughed. She was so small, the flowers around her seemed like trees.

Kirsty twisted round to look at her back. She had wings — shiny and delicate as a butterfly's! Ruby beamed at them. "Now you can fly," she said. "Let's go."

Rachel twitched her shoulders. Her wings fluttered, and she felt herself rise up into the air. She felt quite wobbly at first. It was very odd!

"Help!" Kirsty yelled, as she shot up into the air. "I'm not very good at this!"

"Come on," said Ruby, taking their hands. "I'll help you." She led them up, out of the glade.

Rachel looked down on Rainspell Island. She could see the cottages next to the beach, and the harbour.

"Where *is* Fairyland, Ruby?" Kirsty asked. They were flying higher and higher, up into the clouds.

"It's so far away, that no mortal could ever find it," Ruby said.

They flew on through the clouds for a long, long time. But at last Ruby turned to them and smiled. "We're here," she said.

As they flew down from the clouds, Kirsty and Rachel saw places they recognised from the pond picture: the palace, the hillsides with their toadstool houses, the river and flowers. But there were no bright colours now. Because of Jack Frost's spell, everything was a drab shade of grey. Even the air felt cold and damp.

A few fairies walked miserably across
the hillsides. Their wings hung limply
down their backs. No one could
be bothered to fly.

Suddenly, one of the fairies looked up
into the sky. "Look!" she shouted. "It's
Ruby. She's come back!"

At once, the fairies flew up towards Ruby, Kirsty and Rachel. They circled around them, looking much happier, and asking lots of questions.

"Have you come from Rainspell, Ruby?"

"Where are the other Rainbow Fairies?"

"Who are your friends?"

"First, we must see the King and Queen. Then I will tell you everything!" Ruby promised.

King Oberon and Queen Titania were seated on their thrones. Their palace was as grey and gloomy as everywhere else in Fairyland. But they smiled warmly when Ruby arrived with Rachel and Kirsty.

"Welcome back, Ruby," the Queen said. "We have missed you."

"Your Majesties, I have found two mortals who believe in magic!" Ruby announced. "These are my friends, Kirsty and Rachel."

Quickly Ruby explained what had happened to the other Rainbow Fairies. She told everyone how Rachel and Kirsty had rescued her.

"You have our thanks," the King told them. "Our Rainbow Fairies are very special to us."

"And will you help us to find Ruby's Rainbow sisters?" the Queen asked.

"Yes, we will," Kirsty said.

"But how will we know where to look?" Rachel wanted to know.

"The trick is not to look too hard," said Queen Titania. "Don't worry. As you enjoy the rest of your holiday, the magic you need to find each Rainbow Fairy will find *you*. Just wait and see."

King Oberon rubbed his beard thoughtfully. "You have six days of your holiday left, and six fairies to find," he said. "A fairy each day. That's a lot of fairy-finding. You will need some special help." He nodded at one of his footmen, a plump frog in a buttoned-up jacket.

The frog hopped over to Rachel and
Kirsty and handed them each a tiny,
silver bag.

"The bags contain magic tools," the
Queen told them. "Don't look inside
them yet. Open them only when you
really need to, and you will find
something to help you." She smiled at
Kirsty and Rachel.

"Look!" shouted another frog footman suddenly. "Ruby is beginning to fade!"

Rachel and Kirsty looked at Ruby in horror. The fairy was growing paler before their eyes. Her lovely dress was no longer red but pink, and her golden hair was turning white.

"Jack Frost's magic is still at work," said the King, looking worried. "We cannot undo his spell until the Rainbow Fairies are all together again."

"Quickly, Ruby!" urged the Queen. "You must return to Rainspell at once."

Ruby, Kirsty and Rachel rose into the air, their wings fluttering.

"Don't worry!" Kirsty called, as they flew higher. "We'll be back with all the Rainbow Fairies very soon!"

"Good luck!" called the King and Queen.

Rachel and Kirsty watched Ruby worriedly as they flew off. But as they got further away from Fairyland, Ruby's colour began to return. Soon she was bright and sparkling again.

They reached Rainspell at last. Ruby
led Rachel and Kirsty to the clearing
in the wood, and they landed
next to the old, black pot.
Then Ruby scattered
fairy dust over
Rachel and Kirsty.
There was a puff of
glittering red smoke,
and the two girls
shot up to their
normal size again.
Rachel wriggled
her shoulders. Yes,
her wings had gone.
"Oh, I really *loved*
being a fairy," Kirsty said.
They watched as Ruby sprinkled her
magic dust over the old, black pot.

"What are you doing?" Rachel asked.

"Jack Frost's magic means that I can't help you look for my sisters," Ruby replied sadly. "So I will wait for you here, in the pot-at-the-end-of-the-rainbow."

Suddenly the pot began to move. It rolled across the grass, and stopped under the weeping willow tree. The tree's branches hung right down to the ground.

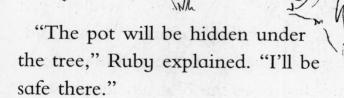

"The pot will be hidden under the tree," Ruby explained. "I'll be safe there."

"We'd better start looking for the other Rainbow Fairies," Rachel said to Kirsty. "Where shall we start?"

Ruby shook her head. "Remember what the Queen said," she told them. "The magic will come to you." She flew over and sat on the edge of the pot. Then she pushed aside one of the willow branches and waved at Rachel and Kirsty. "Goodbye, and good luck!"

"We'll be back soon, Ruby," Kirsty promised.

"We're going to find all your Rainbow sisters," Rachel said firmly. "Just you wait and see!"

Now it's time for Kirsty and Rachel to help...

Amber the Orange Fairy

Read on for a sneak peek...

"What a lovely day!" Rachel Walker shouted, staring up at the blue sky. She and her friend, Kirsty Tate, were running along Rainspell Island's yellow, sandy beach. Their parents walked a little way behind them.

"It's a *magical* day," Kirsty added. The two friends smiled at each other.

Rachel and Kirsty had come to Rainspell Island for their holidays. They had soon found out it really *was* a magical place!

As they ran, they passed rock pools that shone like jewels in the sunshine.

Rachel spotted a little *splash!* in one of the pools. "There's something in there, Kirsty!" she pointed. "Let's go and look."

The girls jogged over to the pool and crouched down to see.

Kirsty's heart thumped as she gazed into the crystal clear water. "What is it?" she asked.

Suddenly, the water rippled. A little brown crab scuttled sideways across the sandy bottom and vanished under a rock.

Kirsty felt disappointed. "I thought it might be another Rainbow Fairy," she said.

"So did I, "Rachel sighed. "Never mind. We'll keep on looking."

"Of course we will," Kirsty agreed. Then she put her finger to her lips as their parents came up behind them.

Kirsty and Rachel had a big secret. They were helping to find the Rainbow Fairies. Thanks to Jack Frost's wicked spell, the fairies were lost on Rainspell Island. And until they were all found there would be no colour in Fairyland.

Rachel looked at the shimmering blue sea. "Shall we have a swim?" she asked...

Read Amber the Orange Fairy to find out what adventures are in store for Kirsty and Rachel!

Meet the
Rainbow Fairies

Ruby
the Red
Fairy

Amber
the Orange
Fairy

Saffron
the Yellow
Fairy

Fern
the Green
Fairy

Sky
the Blue
Fairy

Izzy
the Indigo
Fairy

Heather
the Violet
Fairy

**Also available
as an ebook**

Collect the seven original Rainbow Magic Fairies
to find out how the adventure began!

www.rainbowmagicbooks.co.uk

RAINBOW magic®

Meet the fairies, play games
and get sneak peeks at
the latest books!

There's fairy fun for everyone at

www.rainbowmagicbooks.co.uk

You'll find great activities, competitions, stories and
fairy profiles, and also a special newsletter.

Win Rainbow Magic Goodies!

There are lots of Rainbow Magic fairies, and we want to know which one is your favourite! Send us a picture of her and tell us in thirty words why she is your favourite and why you like Rainbow Magic books. Each month we will put the entries into a draw and select one winner to receive a Rainbow Magic Sparkly T-shirt and Goody Bag!

Send your entry on a postcard to Rainbow Magic Competition, Orchard Books, 338 Euston Road, London NW1 3BH. Australian readers should email: childrens.books@hachette.com.au New Zealand readers should write to Rainbow Magic Competition, PO Box 3255, Shortland St, Auckland 1140, NZ. Don't forget to include your name and address. Only one entry per child.

Good luck!

Meet the
Weather Fairies

Crystal
the Snow
Fairy

Abigail
the Breeze
Fairy

Pearl
the Cloud
Fairy

Goldie
the Sunshine
Fairy

Evie
the Mist
Fairy

Storm
the Lightning
Fairy

Hayley
the Rain
Fairy

Also available
as an ebook

Join Rachel and Kirsty as they hunt for the
feathers that naughty Jack Frost has stolen
from Doodle the magic weather-vane cockerel!

www.rainbowmagicbooks.co.uk